GREAT GAMES

SHARP KiDS

SUPER ACTIVITIES, PUZZLES & GAMES

BY DAVID SMITH

ILLUSTRATED BY MONIKA BODNAR

Watermill Press

10 9 8 7 6 5 4 3

An Amazing Maze

Help this little bunny get through the top hat maze. But, hurry! He is the star of the magic act, and the show is about to begin!

START

FINISH

answer on page 44

3

A Secret Meeting

Coded Message

Jan has written a letter to her friend George. But it is in secret code! Can you help George complete each letter by drawing one line, and read the message?

answer on page 44

Pencil Pets

Word-Find Puzzle

There are 10 little pets hiding in the word-find puzzle below. Can you find them all? One is already circled for you! Words run across and down.

```
G U I N E A P I G O Y I I D C
E B L Q P A L H H M S E Y O Z
R J T H O O A G U L N N R G A
B I M R S P X H A N A D R D J
I (C A N A R Y) F M G K Y B C H
L A G V Z T O A N B E C S O A
O T M C T U R T L E B U E K M
K A D Z J T E B V F M F S P S
W L O Y X P A R A K E E T E T
I M U H D K L N N F D P B G E
G O L D F I S H E E O I R L R
```

CANARY   GOLDFISH   PARAKEET
CAT   GUINEA PIG   SNAKE
DOG   HAMSTER   TURTLE
GERBIL   answer on page 44   5

Silly Scribbles

Can you make an anthill into a cleaning lady scrubbing the floor? It's easy!

Anthill

Cleaning Lady

Now it's your turn to try!

Make a 9 into a funny face.

Make a doughnut into an egg in a frying pan.

Doodle Art

Make an E into a window.

Make a flagpole into a sailboat.

Make a figure 8 into a pair of glasses.

answer on page 44

Every body into the WATER

Did you know that there are eight mammals that like the ocean better than dry land? Although they all breathe air, they spend most of their time in the water. The crossword puzzle is all about them. One Down and Four Across are done for you!

ACROSS

2. The Atlantic _____ .
4. A funny-looking sea mammal.
5. Ocean "cat."
6. The biggest animal in the world!
7. A baby seal.
8. What ocean mammals and fish all can do.
9. A dolphin's close relative.

DOWN

1. This animal likes to eat plants.
3. Walruses come out of the water to lie in the _____ .
4. A porpoise's close relative.
5. It can balance a ball on its nose.
6. It has very long tusks and whiskers.
8. Another name for ocean.
10. Walruses play on _____ bergs.

8

answer on page 45

9

UFO Puzzle

These little spacemen just flew in from Mars.
Can you tell which two are the same?
Draw a circle around them.

answer on page 45

Connect-the-Dots

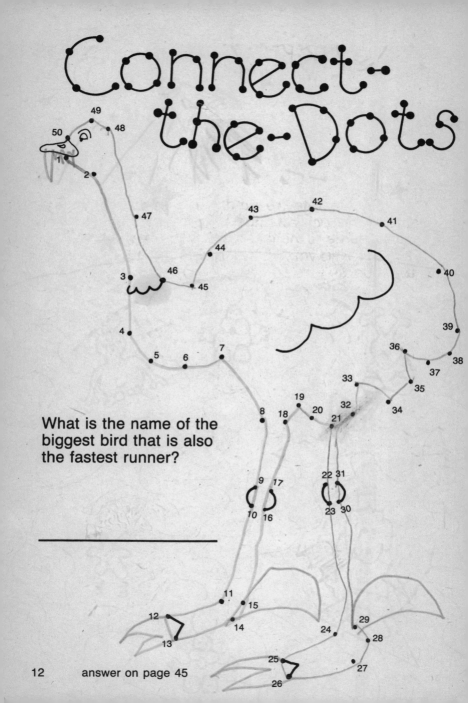

What is the name of the biggest bird that is also the fastest runner?

_____

answer on page 45

WHEEL OF FORTUNE

Can you complete the word wheel below? Fill in the name of each object under its picture. The last letter of each name is the first letter of the next name. Can you make your own word wheel? It is harder than it looks!

answer on page 45

AN INVENTIVE PUZZLE

What do these silly machines do?
Just about anything you can think of!
Can you tell which two silly
machines below are the same?
Draw a circle around them.

answer on page 45

One, Two, Three...

Ten little monkeys are hiding in the tree below.
Can you circle them all?

answer on page 46

What Nonsense!

Scrambled Sayings Puzzle

SHH! ZZZ

SLEEPING LIE DOGS LET!

FLOWERS BRING
MAY SHOWERS APRIL!

Can you make sense of these nonsense sentences?
They are sayings you may know!

THE GREENER ALWAYS ON
THE SIDE IS OTHER GRASS!

_____

_____

UP MUST GOES WHAT DOWN COME!

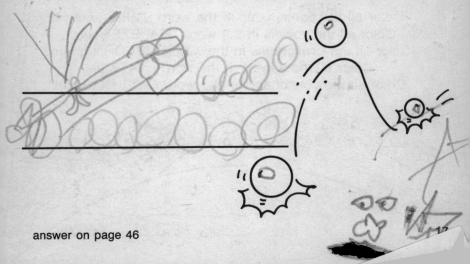

_____

_____

answer on page 46

Color Me Happy

Color-by-Letters Picture

The circus is coming to town!
Color all the spaces on the tent according
to the key, and meet the star of the show!

Color all the consonants in the word SMILE orange.
Color all the vowels in the word TRAPEZE yellow.
Color all the consonants in the word POPCORN green.
Color all the vowels in the word LION blue.
Color all the consonants in the words HOT DOG red.

CIRCUS TODAY!

answer on page 46

Fill-In Puzzle

1. What flower
   should be in
   the zoo?

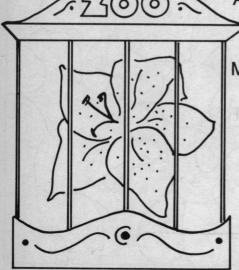

PLAN__

    G_RAFFE

   CA__E

LEAV_S

    G_OWL

ANIMA_S

   GOR_LLA

   B_OOM

MONKE__

The answer is

_____

To find the answers to these "blooming" riddles, fill in the blanks!

2. What flower do you wear everyday?

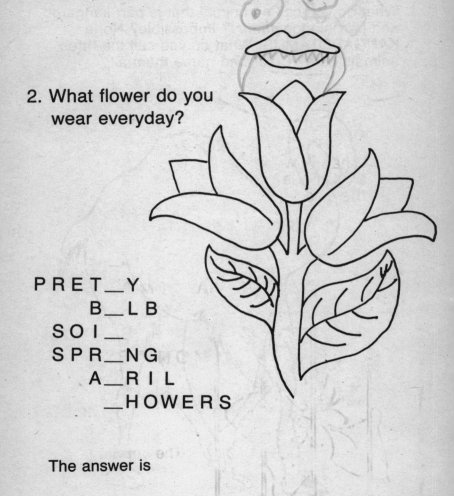

P R E T _ Y
B _ L B
S O I _
S P R _ N G
A _ R I L
_ H O W E R S

The answer is

_____

answer on page 46

Wha·Cha·Ma·Call·It

What do you call an animal that is part kangaroo and part hippopotamus? Impossible? No, a KANGAROTAMUS! What do you call the three animals here? Color and name them all.

1._____

Make up a story about each animal. Is it nice? Is it mean? Does it growl? Does it scream?

2. _____

3. _____

answer on page 46

Ride 'em Cowboy
Puzzle

These cowboys are ready to jump on their horses and ride off into the sunset. Draw each cowboy's path with your pencil. Can you get each cowboy to his own horse without crossing any other lines or going outside the corral?

answer on page 47

PEEK-A-BOO

WORD-FIND PUZZLE

```
H C F X Y U S V L A L Z T
I H O P S C O T C H E S S
D E O U L A C R O S S E E
E C T Q X N C W Y M Z F B
A K B A S K E T B A L L A
N E A Q V W R R Z R B U S
D R L P F M Q M T B Z X E
S S L K I C K B A L L Z B
E P I N G P O N G E U V A
E Q P G L J A C K S L Y L
K B J U M P R O P E Y M L
```

26   answer on page 47

There are 15 games hiding in
the word-find puzzle.
Can you find them all? One
is already circled for you!
Words run across and down.

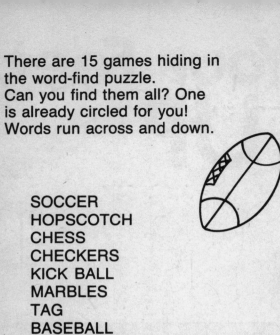

SOCCER
HOPSCOTCH
CHESS
CHECKERS
KICK BALL
MARBLES
TAG
BASEBALL
JUMP ROPE
FOOTBALL
HIDE-AND-SEEK
JACKS
PING-PONG
BASKETBALL
LACROSSE

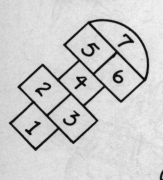

Put Your Feet UP

At this Japanese restaurant customers must take off their shoes before they eat. The people below have gotten their shoes all mixed up! Can you match each person to his or her shoes?

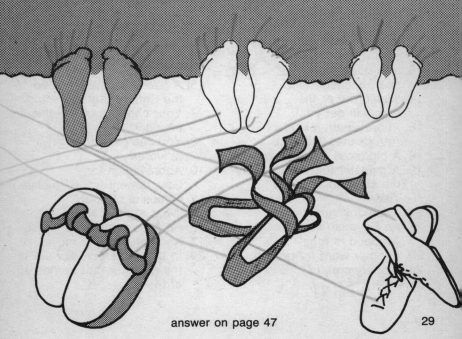

LIFE GUARD

answer on page 47

Step into my parlor

A Monstrous Crossword Puzzle...

Can you do this crossword puzzle? It's lots of fun, but watch out—it's full of scary creatures! Nine Across and Eight Down are done to get you started.

BEWARE: Don't do this puzzle when the moon is full!

ACROSS

4. When the moon is full, this guy becomes a hairy beast!
5. A manmade monster.
9. Even if you have never seen a monster, you can _____ .
12. A name that rhymes with sing.
13. You go to the _____ to see a monster film.
14. Watch out or the _____-man will get you!
16. Abbreviation for New Hampshire. (Initials.)
18. A big mass of icky ooze.
19. A monster that came out of the sea and attacked Tokyo.
21. A famous vampire.
22. An Egyptian monster wrapped in rags.
23. Another word for rescue.
24. A scary creature.

DOWN

1. Usually seen wearing a white sheet.
2. Monsters are _____ and nasty.
3. If you are frightened by the monster movie, you might _____ .
4. The good guys always _____ .
6. A giant ape that climbed the Empire State Building.
7. Your chances of meeting a monster.
8. You can't see this guy. (2 words.)
10. Abbreviation for Government Issue. (Initials.)
11. Opposite of "out."
14. What a ghost says.
15. Another name for a ghost.
17. Another word for movie.
20. In the cemetery, beware of the monster that comes out of the _____ .

answer on page 47

Across: 9. IMAGINE

Down: 8. INVISIBLE MAN

SPOOKY HIDDEN PICTURE

PUZZLE

There are 10 little goblins hiding in the haunted house on the next page. Can you find them all?

answer on page 48

33

A Secret Coded Message...

Here's a joke for you. Can you figure out the code and read the joke? HINT: Fill in the letters of the alphabet on the two lines below. On the first line write the letters forward, and on the second line write the alphabet backward!

ABC _____ XYZ

ZYX _____ CBA

● ● ●   ● ● ●   ◢ ● ●   ◢ ● ●   ◢ ● ●

SLD   LUGVM   WL   BLF   UVVW   Z

GSIVV   SFMWIVW   KLFMW

TLIROOZ ?

ZH   LUGVM   ZH   SV   DZMGH !

---

answer on page 48   35

Matching puzzle

These astronauts mixed up their shadows on the moon. Can you match each astronaut to his own shadow?

What Nonsense!

Scrambled Sayings Puzzle

AN DOG TEACH OLD YOU
CAN'T TRICKS NEW!

_____

A DOCTOR KEEPS THE
DAY AN APPLE AWAY!

_____

_____

Can you make sense of these nonsense sentences?
They are sayings you may have heard before.
(Hint: Look at the illustrations for clues.)

LINING HAS
EVERY SILVER
A CLOUD!

LITTLE OAKS ACORNS
BIG GROW FROM!

answer on page 48

Color-by-Numbers
Picture

There is something hiding in the picture on the next page! Color the spaces according to the key, and find out what is there!

14 = GREEN   17 = BROWN
21 = BLACK   11 = RED

answer on page 48

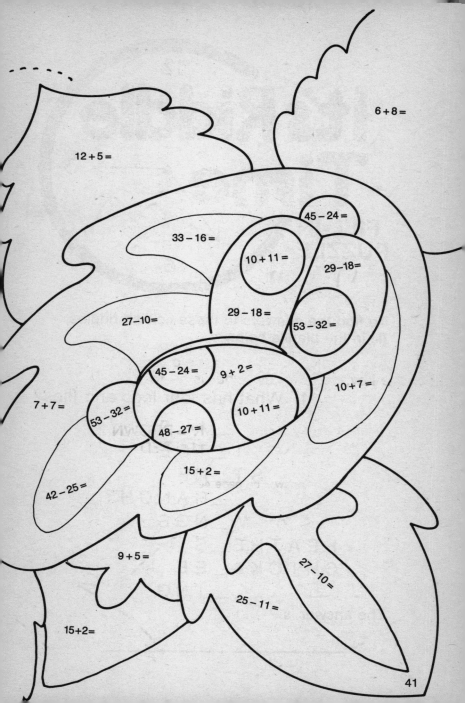

$6 + 8 =$

$12 + 5 =$

$45 - 24 =$

$33 - 16 =$

$10 + 11 =$

$29 - 18 =$

$27 - 10 =$

$29 - 18 =$

$53 - 32 =$

$45 - 24 =$ $9 + 2 =$

$7 + 7 =$

$53 - 32 =$

$10 + 11 =$

$10 + 7 =$

$48 - 27 =$

$15 + 2 =$

$42 - 25 =$

$9 + 5 =$

$27 - 10 =$

$25 - 11 =$

$15 + 2 =$

41

It's Riddle Time

FILL-IN PUZZLE

To find the answers to these ticklish riddles,
fill in the blanks below!

1. What has four legs and flies?

```
  __A I L S
  T __ I C E
  S T __ N E
  __ R A N C H
  W __ N G S
F E A T H E __ S
C H I C K A __ E E
  __ I N G
```

The answer is

_____

2. What bird can lift the heaviest weight?

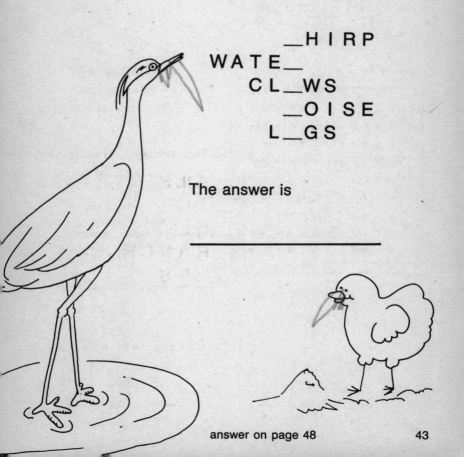

_ H I R P
W A T E _
C L _ W S
_ O I S E
L _ G S

The answer is

_____

answer on page 48

answer for p. 3

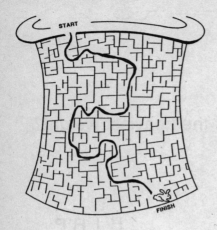

answer for p. 4

HI

MEET ME AT
TEN BY THE
TREE NEAR
THE POND
ON FRIDAY.

JAN

answer for p. 5

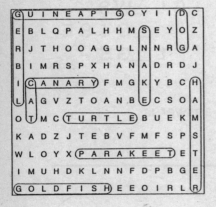

answer for pp. 6-7

Make a 9 into a funny face.

Make a doughnut into an egg in a frying pan.

Make an E into a window.

Make a flagpole into a sailboat.

Make a figure 8 into a pair of glasses.

44

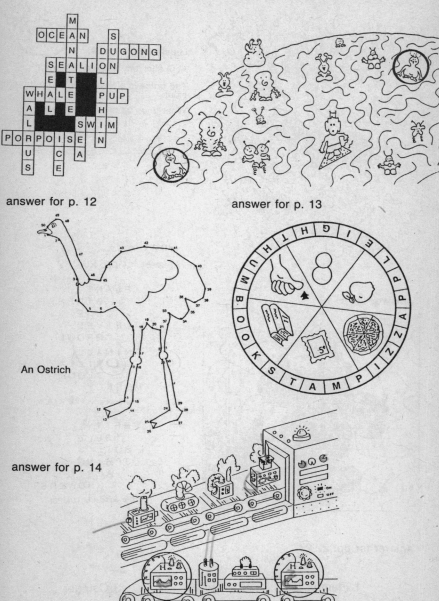

answer for p. 9

answer for pp. 10-11

answer for p. 12

An Ostrich

answer for p. 13

answer for p. 14

45

answer for p. 15

answer for pp. 16-17

Let sleeping dogs lie!

April showers bring May flowers!

The grass is always greener on the other side!

What goes up must come down!

answer for p. 19

answer for pp. 20-21

```
PLANT
    GIRAFFE
    CAGE
LEAVES
    GROWL
ANIMALS
    GORILLA
    BLOOM
MONKEY
```
The answer is TIGER LILY!

```
PRETTY
    BULB
SOIL
SPRING
    APRIL
    SHOWERS
```
The answer is TULIPS!

answer for pp. 22-23

1. Flamamel   2. Elephale   3. Ostriger

answer for p. 25

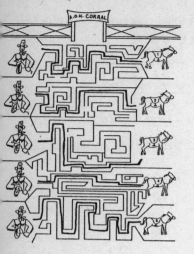

answer for p. 26

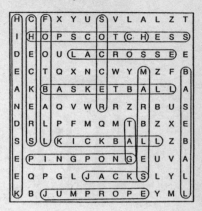

A word search grid:

```
H C F X Y U S V L A L Z T
I H O P S C O T C H E S S
D E O U L A C R O S S E E
E C T Q X N C W Y M Z F B
A K B A S K E T B A L L A
N E A Q V W R R Z R B U S
D R L P F M Q M T B Z X E
S L K I C K B A L L Z B
E P I N G P O N G E U V A
E Q P G L J A C K S L Y L
K B J U M P R O P E Y M L
```

answer for pp. 28-29

answer for p. 30

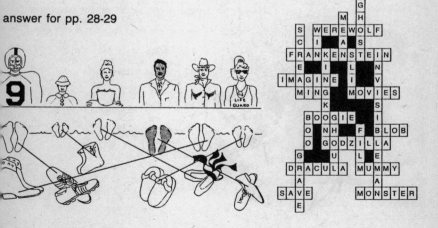

A crossword grid with answers:

GH
M
SCI WEREWOLF
FRANKENSTEIN
IMAGINE NV
MING MOVIES
BOOGIE
ONH BLOB
GODZILLA
DRACULA MUMMY
SAVE MONSTER

47

answer for p. 33

answer for p. 37

answer for pp. 34-35

ABC DEFGHIJKLMNOPQRSTUVWXYZ
ZYXWVUTSRQPONMLKJIHGFEDCBA

SLD LUGVM WL BLF UVVW Z
HOW OFTEN DO YOU FEED A

GSIVV SFMWIVW KLFMW
THREE HUNDRED POUND

TLIROOZ?
GORILLA?

ZH LUGVM ZH SV DZMGH!
AS OFTEN AS HE WANTS!

answer for pp. 38-39

You can't teach an old dog new tricks!
An apple a day keeps the doctor away!
Every cloud has a silver lining!
Big oaks from little acorns grow!

answer for p. 41

Two ladybugs

answer for pp. 42-43

```
     TAILS
    TWICE
   STONE
     BRANCH
    WINGS
 FEATHERS
CHICKADEE
      SING
```

The answer is TWO BIRDS!

```
        CHIRP
 WATER
   CLAWS
       NOISE
    LEGS
```

The answer is a CRANE!